JANIE BYNUM

Altoona Baboona

VOYAGER BOOKS · HARCOURT, INC.

San Diego   New York   London

www.harcourt.com

First Voyager Books edition 2002
Voyager Books is a trademark of Harcourt, Inc., registered in
the United States of America and/or other jurisdictions.

The Library of Congress has cataloged the hardcover edition as follows:
Bynum, Janie K.
Altoona Baboona/Janie Bynum.
p. cm.
Summary: Altoona Baboona travels the world in her hot air balloon.
[1. Baboons—Fiction.   2. Hot air balloons—Fiction.   3. Stories in rhyme.]   I. Title.
PZ8.3.B9935Al   1999
[E]—dc21   98-15889
ISBN 0-15-201860-3
ISBN 0-15-216404-9 pb

A C E G H F D B

The illustrations in this book were done in digital pen and ink and watercolor.
The display type was hand lettered by Janie Bynum.
The text type was set in Berkeley Old Style.
Color separations by Bright Arts Ltd., Hong Kong
Manufactured by South China Printing Company, Ltd., China
Production supervision by Sandra Grebenar and Wendi Taylor
Designed by Linda Lockowitz

For Altoonas everywhere—
And especially for
Taylor, Logan, and Baron

Altoona Baboona
flicks peas with a spoon-a.

She dances all night
and sings songs to the moon-a.

Altoona Baboona
gets bored on her dune-a.

She takes to the skies
in her hot air balloon-a.

Altoona Baboona
flies south to Cancun-a.

She tries to touch down

but blows east to Rangoon-a.

Altoona Baboona
spies a little lost loon-a.

She offers a lift
to the nearest lagoon-a.

Altoona Baboona
hears a toe-tappin' tune-a.

She steers toward the sound. . . .

It's a jazzy raccoon-a!

Altoona Baboona
heads home late in June-a.
She flies way up high
to avoid a monsoon-a.

Altoona Baboona
then lands her balloon-a.

She unpacks her bags
the entire afternoon-a.

Altoona Baboona
flicks peas with a spoon-a.

She dances all night
and sings songs to the moon-a.

But Altoona Baboona—
she now shares her dune-a,
her heart and her home,
with Raccoon-a and Loon-a.